DATE DUE

JA 17 '15			
FE 17 '15			
MR 03 '15			
MR 18 '15			
JY - - '15			
FE 25 '19			
			PRINTED IN U.S.A.

For Enys and Liana – M.E.

WWW.ENCHANTEDLIONBOOKS.COM

First American edition published in 2014 by Enchanted Lion Books
351 Van Brunt Street, Brooklyn, NY 11231
Copyright © 2013 by Kaléidoscope
Originally published in France as LE JOUR OÙ J'AI PERDU MES SUPERPOUVOIRS
Translated from the French by Claudia Bedrick & Kris Di Giacomo
Copyright © 2014 by Enchanted Lion Books for the English-language edition
Translation copyright © 2014 Enchanted Lion Books
All rights reserved under International and Pan-American Copyright Conventions
A CIP record is on file with the Library of Congress
ISBN: 978-1-59270-144-5. Printed in December 2013 by South China Printing Company

Michaël Escoffier
Kris Di Giacomo

THE DAY I LOST MY SUPERPOWERS

ENCHANTED LION BOOKS
NEW YORK

THE DAY I DISCOVERED I COULD FLY,
I KNEW THAT I WAS SPECIAL.

So I STARTED PRACTICING NONSTOP
TO DEVELOP MY SUPERPOWERS.

I HAD A FEW SETBACKS AT THE START...

Woosh

BUT I WORKED HARD
AND GOT BETTER AND BETTER.

MY FAVORITE SUPERPOWER IS MAKING THINGS DISAPPEAR.
ALL I HAVE TO DO IS CONCENTRATE...

AND POOF!
GONE!

SADLY, IT DOESN'T ALWAYS WORK.

I ALSO LIKE GOING
THROUGH WALLS...

PUPPET
SHOW
3 PM

...WALKING ON THE CEILING...

...AND BECOMING INVISIBLE.

When I get bored I try new things. Like communicating with animals.

So far, I've been most successful with plants.

SOMETIMES I THINK THAT I'M PROBABLY
NOT EVEN HUMAN AND I MUST COME FROM
ANOTHER PLANET.

HOW ELSE CAN YOU EXPLAIN
THAT I CAN BREATHE UNDERWATER...

...MOVE OBJECTS
WITHOUT TOUCHING THEM ...

...AND GO BACK IN TIME?

I ALWAYS WONDERED IF MY PARENTS
COULD TELL—IF THEY KNEW ABOUT
MY SUPERPOWERS.

UNTIL ONE DAY WHEN...

I WAS HAPPILY FLYING AROUND
IN THE BACKYARD,

AND SUDDENLY

SPLAT!

NO MORE SUPERPOWERS!
GONE! FINISHED!

AND THEN MY KNEE STARTED TO HURT
AND I BEGAN TO CRY.

MOM CAME RUNNING.
SHE GAVE ME A MAGIC KISS,
AND THEN YOU KNOW WHAT HAPPENED?
I FELT ALL BETTER (EVEN IF MY KNEE STILL
HURT A LITTLE).

So now, you know what I think?
I think my mom has superpowers too!